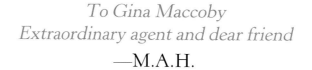

To Gina Maccoby
Extraordinary agent and dear friend
—M.A.H.

To Mel
One of the first of many books created under her care,
encouragement, and love
—M.E.

• Little, Brown and Company • Hachette Book Group • 237 Park Avenue, New York, NY 10017 • Visit our website at www.lb-kids.com • Little, Brown and Company is a division of Hachette Book Group, Inc. • The Little, Brown name and logo are trademarks of Hachette Book Group, Inc. • First Edition: November 2010 • Library of Congress Cataloging-in-Publication Data • Hoberman, Mary Ann. • Very short fables to read together / by Mary Ann Hoberman ; illustrated by Michael Emberley.—1st ed. p. cm.—(You read to me, I'll read to you) • ISBN 978-0-316-04117-1 • 1. Aesop's fables—Adaptations. 2. Children's poetry, American. 3. Fables, American. I. Emberley, Michael, ill. II. Title. • PS3558.O3367V47 2010 811'.54—dc22 • 2009025458 • 10 9 8 7 6 5 4 3 2 1 • SC • Printed in China • The illustrations for this book were done in pencil and watercolor. • The text and display type is Shannon.

Table Of Contents

Author's Note:

Here is another book in the You Read to Me, I'll Read to You series. This time it's a book of fables. Fables are short stories with morals, usually with animals as their characters. The most famous inventor of fables was Aesop, a slave and storyteller who lived in fifth century BC Greece. Many of the stories in this collection are attributed to him.

Unlike those in the previous books, however, the stories here do not end with the familiar refrain "You read to me, I'll read to you." Instead, each one concludes with a moral, which is a brief rule drawn from the story that explains how to act or behave. Some of them are very well known, like "The Country Mouse and the City Mouse" and "The Hare and the Tortoise." Others, like "The Ant and the Dove" and "The Fox and the Stork," may be less familiar. But all of them are fun!

Like the others, this book is for all kinds of readers: young and old, beginning and advanced, individual and group. Whatever the mix, the parts can be switched and the colors exchanged, so that everyone gets a turn to play all the characters.

Once again I salute Literacy Volunteers of America, now merged with Literacy International to form ProLiteracy Worldwide. My work with them inspired these books and continues to inspire me in my efforts to help promote the joy of reading to new readers everywhere.

Introduction

Here's a book
Of Aesop's fables,

    Tales where turtles
    Turn the tables,

Tales with lions,

    Tales with mice,

Tales where ants
Give good advice.

    In this book
    We have two choices

Since each fable
Has two voices.

    You take one voice,
    I, the other;

Then we read
To one another.

    Till we reach
    The fable's moral.

    Then we make
    Our voices choral.

Let's get started—

    One, two, three!

I'll read to you.
You'll read to me.

The Hare and the Tortoise

I'm a tortoise.

    I'm a hare.
    You're a slowpoke.

I don't care.

    You don't care
    That you are slow?

I get where
I want to go.

    I get places
    Really fast.

If we raced,
You'd come in last.

    Come in last?
    I'd lose to you?
    That is silly!

But it's true.

    Well, I dare you—
    Shall we race?

Fine with me.
You choose the place.

    We'll start from here,
    My slowpoke friend.
    The river bridge
    Is where we'll end.

That's fine with me,
My haughty hare.
When you arrive,
You'll find me there.

Off I go—
Just watch my speed!
I must be miles
Into the lead!

One foot, two feet,
Three feet, four—
Keep on going—
Not much more.

Tortoise is
So slow a chap,
I'll just take
A little nap.

Look at Hare—
He's fast asleep!
I'll slip by
Without a peep.

Oh, dear, I fear
That something's wrong!
I bet I slept
A bit too long.

Here comes Hare!
He's drawing near,
But I don't care
Since I am here.

How can this be?
It can't be true!
I am much speedier
Than you!

I know you are,
My silly friend;
But still I beat you
In the end!

Moral: Just keep up an even pace.
Slow and steady wins the race.

The Boy Who Cried Wolf

I am a boy
Who tends some sheep,
A little like
That girl Bo-Peep.

We are some folk
Who live nearby
And every day
We hear his cry.

I cry out "Wolf!"
(It isn't true.)
But they come running.
Yes, they do!

We hear him yell
A wolf is there.
Of course that gives us
Quite a scare.

When they arrive,
Each with a stick,
No wolf is here.
(It's just a trick.)

We're really angry
At his lie;
But every time
We hear his cry,
We think this time
It may be true
So we go running.
Yes, we do.

They scold me and
They say I'm bad.
(It's lots of fun
To make them mad.)

8

The other day
We heard him shout,
"A wolf! A wolf!
A wolf's about!"
This time we said,
"We'll call his bluff.
We just won't go.
We've had enough."

"A wolf! A wolf!
A wolf! It's true!
I need your help!
I really do!"

"That silly boy!
He thinks we're dumb
But we'll show him.
We just won't come."

"A wolf! A wolf!
A wolf's come by!
This time it's true!
It's not a lie!"

Of course we laughed
And did not go.

Of course I cried.
They did not know
This time there really
Was a beast
Who made my flock
Into a feast.

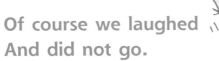

Moral: A liar is rewarded
By the people he's deceived:
Even when he tells the truth,
He will not be believed.

The Ant and the Dove

I am an ant upon a path.
I think I'd like a little bath.
And while I take a bath, I think
I'd also like a little drink.

I am a dove. I love to coo.
I'm in a tree not far from you.

Here's a spring to quench my thirst.
I think I'll drink until I burst!

Oh, dear, the water's racing down!
That little ant's about to drown!

Help! I'm drowning! What a fright!

Help! He's drowning! What a plight!
I'll drop a leaf. The leaf will float
And Ant can use it for a boat.

Look! A leaf from up above!
My life is saved! Oh, thank you, Dove!

Glad to be of help today
And now I shall be on my way.

Oh, goodness me, what do I see?
Someone is behind that tree.
He's catching birds. He's laid a snare
Of sticky twigs. Oh, Dove, beware!

Something's smelling very sweet.
I think it may be good to eat.

I'll give that hunter man a sting
And he will yell like anything!
And when he yells, the dove will flee
And fly away because of me.

What's that yelling in the wood?
It must be bad. It can't be good.
A hunter may be coming near.
I'd better fly away from here.

Moral: You help me and I'll help you.
That's the proper thing to do.
We should always help each other.
One good turn deserves another.

11

The Fox and the Stork

Hello, Miss Stork,
How do you do?

Hello, Sir Fox,
And how are you?

I'm well, Miss Stork.
I'm doing fine.
I wonder if
You'd like to dine?

Why, yes, Sir Fox,
I really would.
A meal with you
Sounds very good.

Well, here we are.
Please take a seat.
I've made some soup
For us to eat.

Just soup for lunch?
You've made us that?
Served in a dish
That's low and flat?
With my long beak
It's plain as day
I cannot eat
A bite today.

Oh, dear, Miss Stork,
What a surprise!
I certainly
Apologize.

(This fox is stingy.
That is clear.
But I'll get even,
Never fear.)

(My scheme has worked!
I planned it right!
She couldn't eat
A single bite!)

My dear Sir Fox,
If you'll agree,
I wish you'd come
And dine with me.

Of course, Miss Stork,
I wouldn't mind.
(A free meal is
My favorite kind!)

Here's our dinner,
Roasted meat.
I hope you get
Enough to eat.

This jug's too slim!
Although I've tried,
I cannot get
My snout inside!

Sir Fox, forgive me
But you see,
A narrow jug's
Just fine for me.

Moral: Turnabout is fair play.
That is what they always say.
If you're mean in what you do,
People will be mean to you.

The Country Mouse and the City Mouse

I'm a little country mouse

        And I am from the city.

Come and see my country house.
Don't you think it's pretty?

        Why, yes, I do, dear Country Mouse.
        It is a lovely sight.
        (I really find it rather plain
        But I must be polite.)

Let's go and have some dinner.
I hope you'll like my food.
(I see she's turning up her nose.
I think that's rather rude.)

        Why, what a lovely dinner!
        A perfect meal for mice!
        (These nuts and seeds are tasteless
        But I'll pretend they're nice.)

We'll stroll across the meadow,
My very favorite spot.
(Oh, dear, she doesn't like it!
It's clear that she does not.)

        I must be leaving, Country Mouse.
        It's time for me to go.
        The country's nice to visit
        But not to live in, no!
        City life is livelier.
        There's more to do and see.
        There's more to eat and more to drink.
        Why don't you visit me?

It certainly sounds wonderful
If all you say is true.
I'll go and pack my suitcase
And come and visit you.

Well, here's the city, Country Mouse!
I told you it was grand.

I've never seen a place like this!
It's just like fairyland!

It's dinnertime, so come with me
And see the splendid spread.
They've left us cheese and cakes and jam.
It's just the way I said.

I've never seen so fine a feast—
But someone's creeping near!
We'll be *his* feast, the horrid beast!
We must get out of here!

Don't worry, Mouse, the cat is gone.
Let's go and get our food.

Not on your life, dear City Mouse!
I am not in the mood.
Exciting as the town may be,
That life does not agree with me.
I've had a thrilling time today
But now I must be on my way.

Moral: Better do with less in cheer
Than live in luxury and fear.

The Dog in the Manger

I am a farm dog
But I'm not a worker.
I lie in the manger.
They call me a shirker.

       I am a helper,
       A hardworking cow.
       I work in the pasture.
       I'm working there now.

How I love napping here
Deep in the hay.
I come in the morning
And stay here all day.

       It's time for my supper.
       I'm ready to eat.
       There's hay in the barn
       So I'm in for a treat.
       But who's in my manger?
       Have I got a guest?
       That lazy old farm dog
       Is taking a rest.

You silly old cow,
I am spending the night.
Do not try to eat
Or I'll give you a bite!

You selfish old dog,
You don't even eat hay.
I'm terribly hungry
So please go away.

No, I will not!
Don't you dare to come near!
I may not eat hay
But I'm staying right here!

That dog is so heartless.
He's mean as can be.
I'll have to go hungry.
No supper for me.

Moral: If something's no use to you,
Stop and take heed.
Don't be like the dog
Who keeps things others need.

The Fox and the Grapes

As I was walking
In the wood,
I spied some grapes.
They looked so good.

Look what we see
Around the bend!
Here comes a fox!
Is this our end?

You lovely grapes,
You smell so sweet.
You're just the thing
I'd like to eat.

That greedy fox,
He likes to steal.
He'd love to have us
For his meal.

You pretty grapes,
You're quite a bunch.
I think I'll munch you
For my lunch.

Oh, here he comes!
He's getting near!
He's right below our vine!
He's here!

I'm right below
And there you are!
But I can't reach!
You're up too far!

The fox can't reach us!
Glory be!
We all are saved!
We still are free!

Those grapes are sour.
I won't stay.
I didn't want them
Anyway.

Moral: When you cannot have a share,
Don't pretend you do not care.
If it's sour grapes you're crying,
Everyone will know you're lying.

19

The Peacock and the Crane

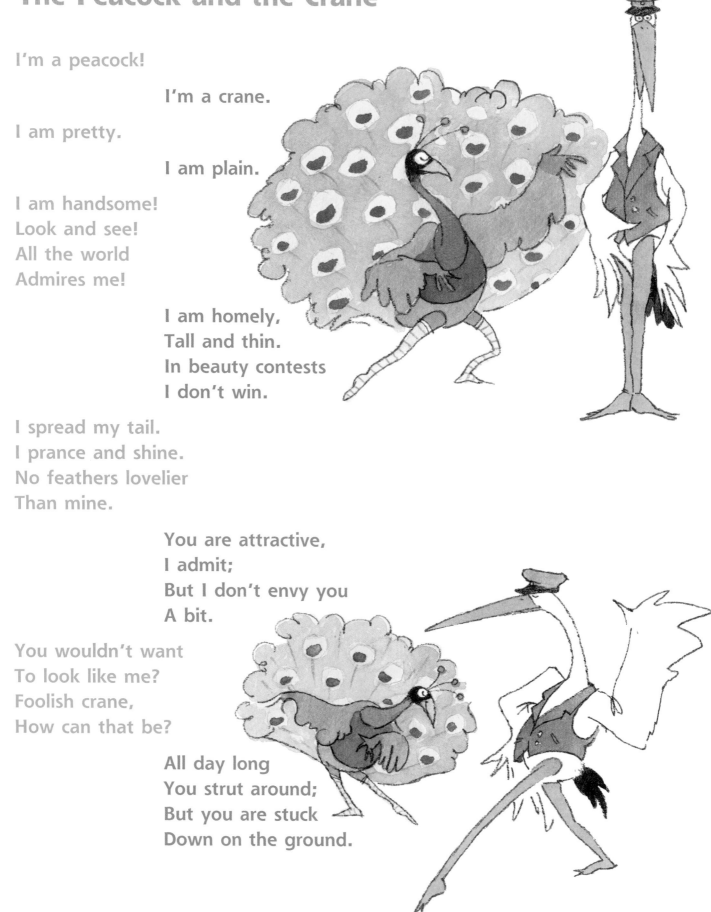

I'm a peacock!

      I'm a crane.

I am pretty.

      I am plain.

I am handsome!
Look and see!
All the world
Admires me!

      I am homely,
      Tall and thin.
      In beauty contests
      I don't win.

I spread my tail.
I prance and shine.
No feathers lovelier
Than mine.

      You are attractive,
      I admit;
      But I don't envy you
      A bit.

You wouldn't want
To look like me?
Foolish crane,
How can that be?

      All day long
      You strut around;
      But you are stuck
      Down on the ground.

I am stuck!
What do you mean?
See my feathers,
Gold and green!

What good are they,
Those shiny things?
I may be gray
But I have wings;
And on those wings
I rise and fly.
See me soar
Into the sky!

I flap my feathers,
Bright and blue;
But they won't lift me
After you.

Farewell, fair Peacock,
Proud and vain.
On the ground
You must remain.

Moral: Don't forget what Peacock heard:
Fine feathers do not make the bird.
When high-fliers call your bluff,
Looks alone are not enough.

The Goose Who Laid the Golden Eggs

I was a farmer
Poor and old
Until my goose
Laid eggs of gold.

Every day
I lay just one,
An egg as golden
As the sun.

A golden egg!
An egg for me!
I'm now as happy
As can be!

My master takes
My eggs away
And sells them all
On market day.

I wish my goose
Laid three or four
Instead of one.
I want some more.

I lay as many
As I can.
He has become
A greedy man.

I'll cut her open
And behold
The secret place
She hides her gold.

Oh, Master!
Put away your knife!
It will not help
To take my life!

My goose is dead
And I despair.
I found no treasure
Anywhere.
There's nothing there
To make the gold
And once again
I'm poor and old.

Moral: Be happy with your current store
And don't go grasping after more;
For if you're greedy, foolish friend,
You will have nothing in the end.

The North Wind and the Sun

I'm the North Wind.
I am cold. I am strong.
No one can beat me
When I come along.

I am the Sun.
I am gentle and warm.
That gives me more power
Than coldness or storm.

Silly old Sun,
You are not very bright!
Let's have a contest
To see who is right.

Look down below
At that bundled-up man.
Make him take off his warm coat
If you can.

Of course I can do that!
I'll raise up a squall
And blow off his coat
With no trouble at all.

The more that you blow, Wind,
And show off your might,
The more the man shivers
And pulls his coat tight.

Well, you go and try
Since you think you're so hot!
But if I can't do it,
You surely cannot.

I'll come out right now
From behind this big cloud
And warm the man up.
Look! He's laughing out loud!

So what if he's laughing
And you're shining bright!
He's still got his coat on.
It's still pulled up tight.

But look at him now!
Though I don't want to gloat,
I have made him so hot
He's unbuttoned his coat!

He has taken it off!
You have beaten me, Sun!

So I have, silly Wind!
You have lost! I have won!

Moral: Blow and bluster do not pay.
Gentleness will win the day.

The Grasshopper and the Ant

It's summertime and all day long
I dance my dance and sing my song.

    It's summertime and all the day
    I work so hard and never play.

How foolish of these boring ants!
Why should I work when I can dance?
With all these oats and grain and wheat,
There's lots of food for me to eat!

    I've hidden every seed I got.
    I've stored it in a secret spot.
    When winter comes with snow and ice,
    These seeds of mine will taste so nice.

Oh, dear, the year is growing old.
The days and nights are getting cold.
The grain is gone, the fields are bare.
I can't find dinner anywhere.

    Now that the summer days are past
    And wintertime is here at last,
    How smart I was to think ahead.
    The winds may blow but I'll be fed.

Oh, Ant, I know that you're my friend.
Do you have, please, some seeds to lend?
If you will let me eat my fill,
I'll pay you back, I swear I will.

While I worked hard all summer long,
What did you do? You sang your song!
Well, now it's winter, as you see,
So dance your dance! Don't bother me!

Moral: Dance your dance, but not all day.
You must work as well as play.

27

The Rooster and the Fox

I am a rooster
Up in a tree,
Roosting and resting—
But what do I see?

Good evening, friend Rooster,
Have you heard the news?
A new day is coming!
We've no time to lose!

A new day is coming?
I've not heard a thing.
No one has told me.
What news do you bring?

Why, peace is here, Rooster!
Our arguing ends!
Once we were enemies!
Now we are friends!

You and I friends, Fox?
I friends with you?
I'd really be happy
If that could be true.

I promise you, Rooster,
I never would lie.
Why don't you come down
From your roost way up high?
You'll give me a hug
And I'll give you a kiss.
I promise, friend Rooster,
There's nothing amiss.

Well, all right, friend Fox,
If you swear it is true—
But someone is coming;
Perhaps there are two.

Tell me, friend Rooster,
Tell me who comes?

One dog, then another.
They must be your chums.

Well, so long, friend Rooster,
I'm off to my lair!
I'll see you tomorrow!
I've no time to spare!

Why, Fox, what's the matter?
What is your hurry?
We all are at peace now.
No reason to worry.

Oh, yes, that is true.
I've been spreading the word;
But there's a small chance
That those dogs haven't heard.

He thought he could fool me
And make me his feast;
But I was too smart
For that crafty old beast!

Moral: Although it sounds as good as gold,
Don't trust everything you're told.

The Lion and the Mouse

Look at the lion
Asleep in the shade.
I'll go and tickle him.
I'm not afraid!

What is that tickle
I feel on my snout?
Look, it's a little mouse
Running about!

Lion, oh, Lion,
Forgive me, please do!
Someday I'll do something
Special for you!

You help a lion,
You tiny wee thing?
What in the world
Could you do for a king?

If you don't eat me
And let me go free,
Someday I'll help you.
Just wait and you'll see.

Oh, run along then.
Get out of my sight.
You're hardly worth eating.
You're only a bite.

Thank you, dear Lion,
And don't you forget.
Someday you'll be
Very happy we met.

Time for some dinner.
How hungry I feel.
I must go hunting
To find my next meal.
Help! I am trapped
From my tail to my snout,
Caught in a net
And I cannot get out!

I hear the lion!
Oh, something is wrong!
I think I can help him
Although I'm not strong.
Don't worry, dear Lion!
Never lose hope!
You'll soon be set free
When I chew through the rope!

You've saved me, wee Mouse,
From a horrible death!
I'll be your protector
Until my last breath!

Moral: Strength is fine, but please recall
       Kindness matters most of all.